DEXTER BEXLEY

AND THE BIG BLUE BEASTIE ON THE ROAD

For Andrea

Copyright © Joel Stewart, 2010
First published in Great Britain in 2010 by Doubleday, an imprint of Random House Children's Books,
61-63 Uxbridge Road, London W5 5SA
First published in the United States of America by Holiday House, Inc. in 2010
All Rights Reserved
HOLIDAY HOUSE is registered in the U.S. Patent and Trademark Office.
Printed and Bound in April 2010 at Tien Wah Press, Singapore.
www.holidayhouse.com
First American Edition
1 3 5 7 9 10 8 6 4 2

Library of Congress Cataloging-in-Publication Data
Stewart, Joel.
Dexter Bexley and the Big Blue Beastie on the road / by Joel Stewart.
— 1st American ed.
p. cm.
Summary: Dexter Bexley and the big blue beastie, who have been thrown
out of town because of their loud hooting, encounter a princess
and a dragon in the deep dark forest where they end up.
ISBN 978-0-8234-2292-0 (hardcover)
1. Humorous stories. 2. Monsters—Fiction. 3. Princesses—Fiction. 4. Dragons—Fiction.
I. Title.   PZ7.S84928Df 2010
[E]—dc22
2009041897

DEXTER BEXLEY
AND THE BIG BLUE BEASTIE ON THE ROAD

JOEL STEWART

Holiday House / New York

Dexter Bexley and the Big Blue Beastie hooted

"AND THERE'S SO MUCH HOOTING TO DO,"

said the Big Blue Beastie.

So they hooted

and hooted,

until . . .

they were thrown out of town.

Dexter Bexley and the Big Blue Beastie
in the deep dark forest . . .

hooted,

hooted,

and hooted!

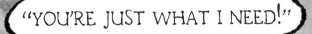

Dexter Bexley and the Big Blue Beastie hooted,

hooted, . . .

and   hooted!

Until . . .

Dexter Bexley

and the Big Blue Beastie

and Princess Philippina

all hooted

together!

Until . . .

"IS IT TIME FOR OUR WEDDING YET?"

asked the tremendously charming Sir Percy Pecket.

Dexter Bexley and the Big Blue Beastie and
Princess Philippina went to slay the Frightful Dragon.

But the Frightful Dragon wasn't really frightful
after all, so Dexter Bexley and the Big Blue Beastie and
Princess Philippina taught him how to tap dance.

The Frightful Dragon had talent.

Dexter Bexley and the Big Blue Beastie and Princess Philippina and the Frightful Dragon became wandering players.

They were a hit.

"YOU'RE NATURALS!"

said the king and the queen and all the king's and queen's advisers.

Dexter Bexley and the Big Blue Beastie and Princess Philippina and the Frightful Dragon wandered

and played

and sang

and told tall tales

from one end of the kingdom to the other.

Then they wandered and played and sang
and told tall tales all the way back . . .

until they stood at the Frightful Dragon's front door.

Luckily, the tremendously charming Sir Percy Pecket arrived and sang the song he'd sung for Princess Philippina on Tuesday.

It was a beautiful lullaby.

Dexter Bexley and the Big Blue Beastie and
Princess Philippina and the Frightful Dragon
stopped to listen.

Then they yawned

and stretched

and . . .

fell wonderfully, silently asleep.

"PHEW!"

Until . . .

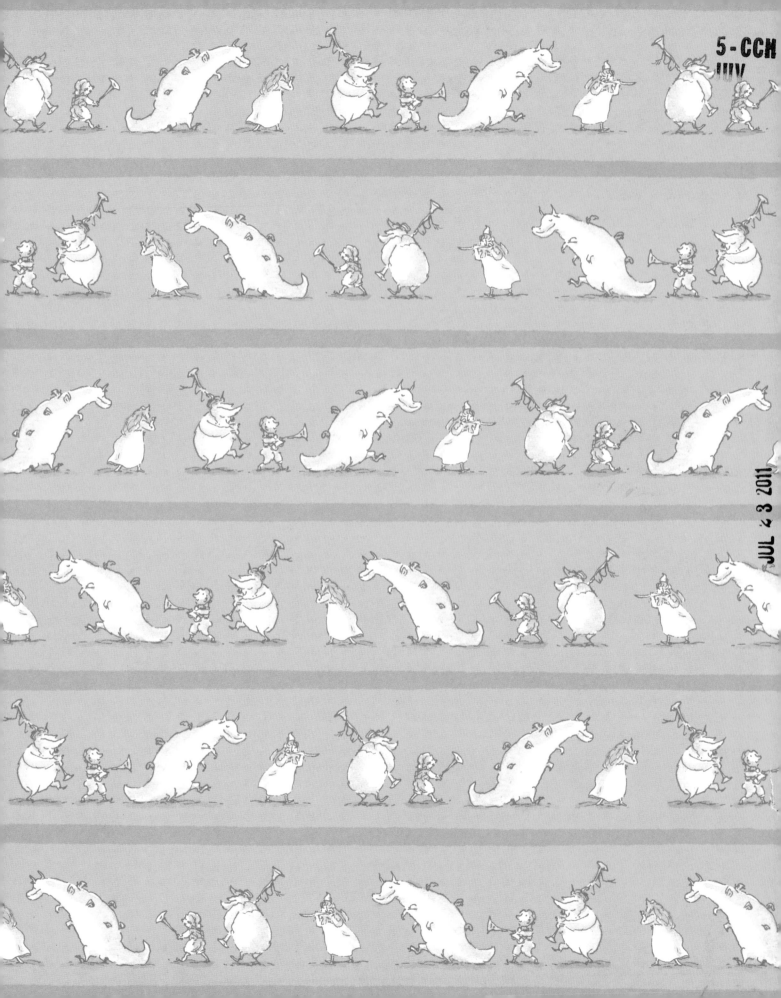